MW01279802

America's Game
California Angels

Jack Cole

ABDO & Daughters
PUBLISHING

Published by Abdo & Daughters, 4940 Viking Dr., Suite 622, Edina, MN 55435.

Copyright ©1997 by Abdo Consulting Group, Inc., Pentagon Tower, P.O. Box 36036, Minneapolis, Minnesota 55435. International copyrights reserved in all countries. No part of this book may be reproduced in any form without written permission from the publisher. Printed in the United States.

Cover photo: Allsport
Interior photos: Wide World Photo, pages 6, 7, 9, 14, 21, 23, 27.
Allsport, pages 5, 17.

Edited by Kal Gronvall

Library of Congress Cataloging–in–Publication Data

Cole, Jack, 1970-
California Angels / Jack Cole
p. cm. — (America's game)
Includes index.
Summary: Details the history of the California Angels, a Los Angeles team that started in 1960.
ISBN 1-56239-676-5
1. California Angels (Baseball team)—Juvenile literature.
[1. California Angels (Baseball team)—History 2. Baseball—History.] I. Title. II. Series.
GV875.C34C65 1997
796.357' 64' 0979494—dc20   96-23778
                                                                          CIP
                                                                          AC

Contents

California Angels

The California Angels have been called All-Stars, baseball's unluckiest team, and baseball's best team on paper. However, unlike their National League counterpart, the Los Angeles Dodgers, they have never been called a winner. In their first 18 seasons the Angels' winning percentage was less than .500, and only once did they finish higher than third place in their division. They finally won the American League (AL) West pennant in 1979. Gene Autry, the Hollywood cowboy who rode the famous horse "Champion," bought the expansion Los Angeles Angels. He knew it would be some time before they would win a pennant, but he never thought it would take 19 years.

Facing page: J.T. Snow, a strong hitter and fielder, represents the Angels' promising future.

Bill Rigney, the Angels' first manager, during spring training.

Building The Team

On December 7, 1960, Gene Autry, a great fan of baseball, became the owner of the new franchise in Los Angeles to be called the Angels. Within 24 hours he had hired Fred Haney as his general manager. Fred Haney was a long-time baseball man who had played on the Detroit Tigers with Ty Cobb.

Hiring a manager was the first order of business for Autry and Haney. Their choice was Bill Rigney, who had managed the New York and San Francisco Giants from 1956 until he was let go midway through the 1960 season.

Bill Rigney knew the Angels didn't have a minor league system. Therefore, the major league team would have to be made up of old or inexperienced players. He realized it would be a struggle, but he accepted the job.

In order to compete with the Dodgers, who had a winning tradition on their side, the Angels needed big-name veterans. At the same time, with no minor league system to draw from, they needed young talent. They decided to go for young talent, and drafted shortstop Jim Fregosi, pitcher Dean Chance, and catcher Bob (Buck) Rodgers.

The first player selected in the first major league expansion draft was a 26-year-old right-handed pitcher named Eli Grba. Grba won the first regular-season game for the Los Angeles Angels.

When the Angels put together their final roster for the 1961 season, critics looked at it and said the team couldn't win 50 games. But the Angels came ready to play—and to prove the critics wrong. The 1961 Angels finished 8th but had won 70 games in their inaugural season, which remains an expansion record.

Eli Grba, the Angels' right-handed pitching ace.

Play Ball!

The Angels played their first season at Wrigley Field in Los Angeles in front of 600,000 fans, far less than the Dodgers' 1.8 million fans down the road at the Los Angeles Coliseum.

Early on, the young Angels showed they had some offensive punch. The young Buck Rodgers, who went back and forth between the big leagues and the minor leagues in 1961, hit .321 for the Angels, while Albie Pearson hit .288. Five players—Ken Hunt, Leon "Daddy Wags" Wagner, Lee "Mad Dog" Thomas, Earl Averill, and Steve Bilko—would each hit 20 or more home runs in 1961.

On May 9, the Angels made their first trade and acquired Ryne "The Flame" Duren, who helped a makeshift bullpen. The bullpen was the foundation for the Angels' 70 wins. In their first season only three pitchers—Ken McBride, Eli Grba, and Ted Bowsfield—won more than 10 games. But the bullpen finished with 34 saves, and helped give the team a respectable 4.31 team ERA. The front office knew starting pitching won pennants, and that would be the subject of off-season moves.

In 1962, the Angels played their home games at Chavez Ravine, also home of the Los Angeles Dodgers. The front office found it tough to compete, playing in the same stadium as the Dodgers.

The Ups
And Downs
Of Pitching

The Angels continued to build with pitchers in 1962. One was Dean Chance, picked up a year earlier in the expansion draft out of the Baltimore Orioles' organization. The second, Robert (Bo) Belinsky, signed as a free agent before the 1962 season, also came from the Baltimore organization.

In the first two months of the season, Bo Belinsky's screwball was nearly unhittable. He began the season winning his first three starts. Then, on May 5, 1962, Belinsky pitched a no-hitter against Baltimore, running his record to 4-0. He was the first to pitch a no-hitter in the new stadium in Los Angeles. A pitcher for the Dodgers named Sandy Koufax would pitch the second no-hitter.

Bo Belinsky fires a screwball during his first start with the Angels in 1962.

Bo won his fifth-straight game to run his record to 5-0, but then fell apart. He finished the season with a 10-11 record and a 3.56 ERA. His career spanned 8 years in the majors, and he only won 28 games. The Angels traded him to the Philadelphia Phillies after the 1964 season.

Dean Chance did not start the 1962 season as well as Belinsky, but was more consistent throughout the year. He finished the season 14-10, had 8 saves and a 2.96 ERA. Two years later Chance, with a 20-9 record and a 1.65 ERA, won the Cy Young Award. Chance pitched five strong seasons for the Angels before being traded to the Minnesota Twins.

The 1962 Angels, anchored by Belinsky and Chance, were in first place on the Fourth of July. They stayed in the thick of the pennant race into August, when luck finally turned against them. In Boston, Art Fowler, an ace out of the bullpen, was hit on the side of the head by a batted ball during batting practice. He lost sight in his left eye, ending his career. The next day Ken McBride, who had won more than 10 games for the second-straight season, broke his rib.

The Angels were still near the leaders into the first weeks of September, finding themselves only $3^1/2$ games behind. They won only 4 of their last 16 games and finished the season in third place at 86-76.

Many Awards, But No Titles

For the 1962 season, "Daddy Wags" was an All-Star, smacking 37 homers and driving in 107 runs. Jim Fregosi led the team with a .291 batting average. Rigney was named the American League's Manager of the Year, and Haney was named Executive of the Year.

The only problem with the 1962 season was that the Angels' front office mistakenly thought they had the makings of a championship team. Instead, the 1963 Angels finished in ninth place at 70-91.

In 1964 they improved to 82-80 and a fifth-place finish. And in 1965, the year the Dodgers won it all, the Angels fell back to below .500 at 75-87 and a seventh-place finish.

A Short Move And A New Name

Since the day they moved into Dodger Stadium, the Angels' front office had been looking for another town to call home. They nearly landed in Long Beach, California, but after serious negotiations only one thing ruined the deal. The city insisted the team be called the Long Beach Angels. Owner Autry, knowing Long Beach would not have national recognition, declined. Soon after the Long Beach negotiations fell through, Anaheim came knocking.

Anaheim, California, was about 50 miles south of Los Angeles with a population at the time of 150,000 people. But all studies showed it was a town with a population about to explode. Anaheim was home to Mickey Mouse and Disneyland. Even more, they didn't care what Autry called his team.

When the first pitch was thrown to start the 1966 season, the Angels played their games in Anaheim Stadium and called themselves the California Angels.

Anaheim Stadium at the time seated 40,000, expanding to 70,000 when the Los Angeles Rams moved there from the Coliseum in 1980. The Stadium's trademark is the Big A scoreboard with a halo around the top of the A that continually flashed after every Angels win. The Big A was moved to the parking lot during the stadium expansion in 1980.

A Decade
Of Disaster

There were very few bright spots between the Angels' first year in Anaheim Stadium and their first pennant in 1979. The team still had no minor league system. In fact, only two everyday players—Carney Lansford and Willie Aikens, of the 1979 team—were brought up through the Angels' system. Even worse, the team suffered many injuries and even death during this period.

In 1967, the Angels acquired a power hitter named Don Mincher from the Minnesota Twins. He led the Angels that year with 25 home runs and 76 RBIs. In early 1968, Mincher was hit by a pitch in a game against the Cleveland Indians. He was never the same hitter, so the Angels traded him away at the end of the 1968 season.

In the off-season of 1968, Minnie Rojas was involved in a car accident. After only three major league seasons, he had collected 23 wins and 43 saves for the Angels. He was permanently paralyzed from the accident, never to pitch again.

In 1973, the Angels acquired a great young hitter named Bobby Valentine, who played both infield and outfield. In the same season, he was chasing down a long fly ball in Anaheim Stadium and crashed into the center field wall. He broke his leg so severely that he was never a regular everyday player again.

In 1977, the Angels signed many free agents to bring in a winner. Two of them, Joe Rudi, an outfielder who had played for the Oakland Athletics, and second baseman Bobby Grich, who had played for Baltimore, were lost for the season due to injuries.

In 1978, the Angels signed more free agents. One was Lyman Bostock, an outfielder from the Minnesota Twins. In September of that year, while visiting family and friends in Gary, Indiana, Bostock was killed.

It seemed the Angels were cursed. Every year they would acquire free agents, make trades, work the waiver wire, and finally put together a competitive group—and still something would go wrong. But the team did acquire one no-nonsense kind of guy, someone who became a bright spot during a bleak period for the California Angels.

Lyman Bostock jumps safely back to first base during a 1978 game against the Kansas City Royals.

No-No Nolan

The best and worst move the Angels made involved a hard-throwing dominant pitcher named Nolan Ryan. On December 11, 1971, the Angels traded aging All-Star shortstop Jim Fregosi, the only player left from the 1961 Angels, to the New York Mets for Nolan Ryan.

In the 1972 season, Ryan started 39 games and pitched 284 innings. He led the majors with 329 strikeouts. Ryan was a soft-spoken Texan who had a business-like approach on the mound. He was the hardest throwing pitcher in baseball, but lacked control. He caused hitters to be back on their heels while attempting to stand in the batter's box. One of the greatest hitters of all, Reggie Jackson, admitted Ryan was the only pitcher he ever feared.

Nolan Ryan finished the season 19-16, with a 2.28 earned run average (ERA) and a league-leading 9 shutouts. The Angels finished a disappointing 75-80, and fifth place in the American League West.

In 1973, Nolan Ryan was the only attraction for an Angels team that again would play under .500, going 79-83. He left many milestones on the 1973 season. It was a season he started 39 games that included 26 complete games and 4 shutouts. Ryan finished the season 21-16 with a 2.87 ERA. Ryan would again lead the majors with 383 strikeouts.

On May 15, 1973, Nolan pitched the first of his major-league-record seven no-hitters. In a game against the Kansas City Royals, Ryan pitched 9 innings, giving up no hits and no errors with 12 strikeouts.

On July 3 of that year, Sal Bando of the Oakland A's stepped in against Nolan Ryan. When Bando left the box he became Ryan's

1,000th career strikeout. Ryan was well on his way to a major-league-record 5,668 strikeouts.

Two weeks later, on July 15 against the Detroit Tigers, Ryan became only the fifth man in history to throw two no-hitters in a single season. Of Nolan's 27 outs, 17 were strikeouts!

From 1974 through 1978, Nolan Ryan added to his legendary status. In five seasons, he led the majors in strikeouts four times. Nolan won over 100 games and pitched 93 complete games during that time.

In August 1974, Ryan had a pitch clocked at 100.9 mph, giving him an entry into the Guinness Book of World Records for the fastest pitch ever thrown. In the final game of the 1974 season, Ryan recorded his third no-hitter with the Angels, beating the Minnesota Twins 4-0. He struck out 15 that day.

In 1975, Ryan tied Sandy Koufax for most career no-hitters when he pitched his fourth no-hitter, beating Baltimore 1-0. On August 31, 1976, Nolan struck out Ron LeFlore for his 2,000th career strikeout. In 1979, Ryan's team-leading 16 wins would help guide the Angels to their first pennant ever.

Former Minnesota Twin hitting great Rod Carew came to the California Angels in 1979.

Autry Builds A Winner

The 1970s brought free agency to baseball. Players meeting certain criteria and whose contracts were expired were no longer the property of the team that first signed them. They were allowed to sign with any team in Major League Baseball.

For owners like Autry, it became an opportunity to put together a championship team. In 1976, he signed free agent Bobby Grich, who became the Angels' everyday second basemen. In 1977, he signed outfielders Don Baylor and Joe Rudi away from the Oakland Athletics. In 1979, he signed one of baseball's best hitters, Rod Carew from the Twins. All would play an important role in the 1979 season.

California

Before becoming the first manager of the Angels in 1961, Bill Rigney managed the New York Yankees and the San Francisco Giants.

In 1961 pitcher Eli Grba won the first regular-season game for the Angels.

Bo Belinsky pitched the first no-hitter in the Angels' new stadium in 1961.

Outfielder and former Minnesota Twin Lyman Bostock joined the Angels in 1978.

Rod Carew, one of
baseball's best
hitters, signed with
the Angels in 1979.

Slugger and former
New York Yankee
Reggie Jackson came
to the Angels in 1982.

Fred Lynn's .517 playoff
batting average is first
among players with 25
or more "at-bats."

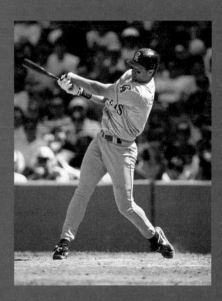

As a balanced hitter and
fielder, J. T. Snow holds
great promise for the
Angels' franchise.

Finally, A Pennant

On September 25, 1979, at Anaheim Stadium, Autry's dream came true. By beating the Kansas City Royals that night 4-1 the Angels clinched their first pennant. During the clubhouse celebration that night, Nolan Ryan said of Autry, "I imagine he's about as happy right now as he can remember being."

As the American League West Champions, the Angles had to get serious. Within two weeks they would meet the Baltimore Orioles for the American League Championship Series (ALCS).

In Game 1 of the ALCS the Angels lost a heartbreaker. Nolan Ryan pitched seven strong innings and left with the game tied 3-3. The game went into extra innings, and in the bottom of the 10th with two on and two out, John Lowenstein homered for a 6-3 victory. Baltimore led the five-game series 1-0.

In Game 2, behind Eddie Murray's single, homer, and four RBIs, the Orioles got off to an early 9-1 lead after three innings. But the Angels would fight hard and score seven runs in the final four innings—only to lose 9-8.

It was back to Anaheim for Game 3. The series was almost over as Baltimore led 3-2 going into the bottom half of the ninth. But California rallied for two runs in their half of the ninth when seldom-used Larry Harlow hit a looping double to drive in the winning run.

The Angels seemed to be back in the series, trailing 2-1 with Game 4 in Anaheim. But the Angels' bats couldn't get going, collecting only six hits in a 6-0 loss. Baltimore won the ALCS 3-1.

Slugger Reggie Jackson smashes a hit against the Chicago White Sox.

Some Down Years

Again the Angels thought they had the makings of a championship team to take them into the 1980s. But the team fell apart in the 1980 season. They finished in sixth place with a 65-95 record, just seven games ahead of the last-place Seattle Mariners. The Angels could never get it going in the strike-shortened season of 1981, finishing 51-59.

After the 1979 championship season, the Angels kept looking in the free-agent market to field the best team. Between 1979 and 1982, the Angels signed outfielder Fred Lynn from the Boston Red Sox, and the great slugger, Reggie Jackson, from the New York Yankees.

This was also when California made its biggest free agent blunder. The Angels thought that Ryan, at 33, had his best years behind him. They decided not to resign him. Nolan pitched 13 more seasons for the Houston Astros and the Texas Rangers, collecting three more no-hitters and nearly 3,000 more strikeouts. But even without Ryan, the Angels were primed for a pennant.

Back In The Playoffs

After the strike-shortened 1981 season, the Angels got off to a great start in 1982, looking like a team of destiny. With star players—including Rod Carew, Don Baylor, Reggie Jackson, and Fred Lynn—the Angels won the American League West with a 93-69 record. They hosted the Milwaukee Brewers for the right to play in the World Series.

In Game 1 of the 1982 ALCS, Don Baylor set a record with five RBIs as the Angels won 8-3 to lead the series 1-0. In Game 2, Reggie "Mr. October" Jackson had a key homer to help the Angels take a 2-0 lead in the series with a 4-2 win.

The series moved to Milwaukee for the final three games. The Brewers gave their fans a treat as they won the next three games to steal the series away from the Angels.

Once again, the Angels missed a chance at a world title and had to return to the drawing board.

Facing page: Angels' outfielder Fred Lynn drives a hit during a 1982 game against the Oakland A's.

Another Disappointing Finish

The Angels finished in fifth place in 1983, with a record of 70-92. In 1984, the Angels' record of 81-81 was good enough for a second-place finish, leaving them three games behind. In 1985, the division and the Angels proved to be much stronger. Their 90-72 finish left them one game behind the division champion Kansas City Royals.

The Angels played the 1986 season with a different attitude, knowing that one game in the regular season can make a difference. In 1986, the Angels won their third pennant in the American League West with a 92-70 record, five games ahead of the Texas Rangers. They would meet the AL Champion Boston Red Sox.

In 1986, the championship series was expanded to seven games. The first game was played in Boston. Mike Witt threw a complete game five-hitter, as the Angels cruised to an 8-1 win. In Game 2, the Angels got sloppy with three errors, which led to three Boston runs. Boston evened the series after winning 9-2.

Back in Anaheim, the Angels won 5-3 and looked great. Game 4 was a tough battle as California was trailing 3-2 going into the bottom of the ninth. The Angels loaded the bases and batter Brian Downing was hit by a pitch. This tied the game and sent it into extra innings. In the bottom of the 11th, Bobby Grich singled in the winning run for an Angels 4-3 victory. The Angels took a commanding 3-1 lead in the ALCS.

The Angels led for most of Game 5 and were ahead 5-2 as they entered the top of the ninth. Mike Witt had pitched eight strong innings but gave up two runs in the top of the ninth before getting two outs. He was relieved by Gary Lucas, who promptly beaned Rich Gedman.

With a man on first, two out, and the score 5-4, Donnie Moore entered the game. He was the Angels' closer who had a great season in 1986, finishing with 21 saves and a 2.97 ERA. One more save for Donnie Moore and the Angels would be headed to the World Series.

Dave Henderson stepped up to the plate for the Red Sox, and quickly fell behind in the count with one ball and two strikes. With the Angels one strike away from their first World Series, the crowd was on their feet. Henderson soon silenced the crowd when he took a 1-2 fork ball from Moore and sent it into the left field bleachers. The two-run homer gave the Red Sox a 6-5 lead, and put the Angels in a state of shock. California did tie the game in the bottom of the ninth with a Rob Wilfong single, sending the game into extra innings. But in the 11th, Henderson's sacrifice fly brought home the winning run, as the Red Sox won 7-6.

Due to Henderson's two-run homer, the disappointed Angels returned to Boston to finish the series instead of heading directly to the World Series.

California, still leading the series 3-2, had nothing left. They were trounced in the final two games. Boston would represent the American League in the World Series, while the Angels had blown their third opportunity at a World Championship.

Back In The Saddle

The collapse in the 1986 playoffs followed the Angels into the 1987 season as they finished last in the American League West with a 75-87 record. Between 1987 and 1992 the Angels never finished higher than third in the AL West, and had only one season where they played above .500. During those years they brought in Whitey Herzog as their general manager. The Angels finally had a GM who could scout young talent. His draft picks during those years gave the Angels the foundation for their future success.

By 1993 some of these draft picks were called up to play in the big leagues. The 1994 season was ruined due to a players strike, and it was hard to tell where the team was headed. Although the 1995 season started late due to the strike, the Angels were a strong team from the start. Players like Tim Salmon, J.T. Snow, Garrett Anderson, and Jim Edmunds were all great hitters and fielders.

California had a great pitcher in Jim Abbott, who was drafted by the Angels, traded to the New York Yankees for J.T. Snow, and then reacquired during the 1994 season. To make sure they didn't have a problem with the closer role, California acquired veteran Lee Smith. The Angels also had a great closing prospect in Troy Percival.

Facing page: Jim Edmunds bats in the 66th All-Star game in Arlington, Texas, July 11, 1995.

California had a terrific season in 1995, led by many young players. The Angels were leading the new American League West well into August. But an injury to star shortstop Gary Disarcina caused their commanding lead to dwindle by September.

The Angels found themselves tied with the Seattle Mariners for first place in the American League West at the end of the regular season. A one-game playoff was played in Seattle's Kingdome. For seven innings the Angels played tough, but could not get anything going against Mariner starting pitcher Randy Johnson. Finally, the Mariners blew it open in the bottom of the seventh and eventually won the game 9-1. The Angels realized once again how important one game could be.

Much like the Angels of 1986, the 1996 team came to play one game at a time. Baseball analyst Steve Sonntag predicted that the 1996 Angels would win the American League West. But again the Angels came up short. Gene Autry will have to continue to wait to ride another "champion" into the sunset.

Glossary

All-Star: A player who is voted by fans as the best player at one position in a given year.

American League (AL): An association of baseball teams formed in 1900 which make up one-half of the major leagues.

American League Championship Series (ALCS): A best-of-seven-game playoff with the winner going to the World Series to face the National League Champions.

Batting Average: A baseball statistic calculated by dividing a batter's hits by the number of times at bat.

Earned Run Average (ERA): A baseball statistic which calculates the average number of runs a pitcher gives up per nine innings of work.

Fielding Average: A baseball statistic which calculates a fielder's success rate based on the number of chances the player has to record an out.

Hall of Fame: A memorial for the greatest baseball players of all time located in Cooperstown, New York.

Home Run (HR): A play in baseball where a batter hits the ball over the outfield fence scoring everyone on base as well as the batter.

Major Leagues: The highest ranking associations of professional baseball teams in the world, currently consisting of the American and National Baseball Leagues.

Minor Leagues: A system of professional baseball leagues at levels below Major League Baseball.

National League (NL): An association of baseball teams formed in 1876 which make up one-half of the major leagues.

National League Championship Series (NLCS): A best-of-seven-game playoff with the winner going to the World Series to face the American League Champions.

Pennant: A flag which symbolizes the championship of a professional baseball league.

Pitcher: The player on a baseball team who throws the ball for the batter to hit. The pitcher stands on a mound and pitches the ball toward the strike zone area above the plate.

Plate: The place on a baseball field where a player stands to bat. It is used to determine the width of the strike zone. Forming the point of the diamond-shaped field, it is the final goal a base runner must reach to score a run.

RBI: A baseball statistic standing for *runs batted in.* Players receive an RBI for each run that scores on their hits.

Rookie: A first-year player, especially in a professional sport.

Slugging Percentage: A statistic which points out a player's ability to hit for extra bases by taking the number of total bases hit and dividing it by the number of at bats.

Stolen Base: A play in baseball when a base runner advances to the next base while the pitcher is delivering his pitch.

Strikeout: A play in baseball when a batter is called out for failing to put the ball in play after the pitcher has delivered three strikes.

Triple Crown: A rare accomplishment when a single player finishes a season leading their league in batting average, home runs, and RBIs. A pitcher can win a Triple Crown by leading the league in wins, ERA, and strikeouts.

Walk: A play in baseball when a batter receives four pitches out of the strike zone and is allowed to go to first base.

World Series: The championship of Major League Baseball played since 1903 between the pennant winners from the American and National Leagues.

Index